# C.C. Downer

## Otis the Flying Goat

From Otis
with Love!

C C Downer

Nightingale Books

NIGHTINGALE PAPERBACK

A CIP catalogue record for this title is
available from the British Library.

ISBN 978-1-78788-217-1

*Nightingale Books is an imprint of
Pegasus Elliot MacKenzie Publishers Ltd.
www.pegasuspublishers.com*

First Published in 2024

**Nightingale Books
Sheraton House  Castle Park
Cambridge  England**

Printed & Bound in Great Britain

## Dedication

Dedicated to my dear friend Otis the goat who lives on a small farm in Aptos, California. He lives his life in joy and belief.

Otis the goat believed he could fly,
though he didn't know how or why...

So he put on some goggles and a long white scarf so that at the least he would look the part.

But Otis still wasn't sure what to do...

But he let out a "BLEAT!"
Kinda like a sheep! Then he took a Running Leap!

And **FLEW!**

UP, UP, UP! Way up into the sky!
And sure enough, THAT GOAT COULD FLY!

He flew over here....

He flew over there...

That silly goat flew everywhere!

He flew from the roof,
then down to the lawn,

where a group of kids
were cheering him on!

"GO OTIS!" they yelled!
"FLY HIGHER!" they screamed.
This flying he thought, is easy it seems...

Next he flew over the garden gate
and truly enjoyed all the veggies he ate!

He flew from the garden just after his snack
And it seemed like he may never have to go back...

He leaped and soared, and he flew some more,
enjoying his birds eye view.
But all good things must come to an end,
and Otis knew this to be true...

So he leaped back into the sky for one last fly
and landed safely back in his pen...

Otis took off his goggles and he took off his scarf,
and became just a goat at THE END